MW00953254

This book belongs to

_____

Amelia Ophelia and Narwally Protectors of the Sea
All Rights Reserved
Text copyright © 2024 by JoAnn M. Dickinson
Illustrations copyright © 2024 by Kerrie Nichols

No part of this book may be reproduced or transmitted, downloaded, distributed, reversed
engineered, or stored in or introduced into any information storage and retrieval system, in any
form or by any means, including photocopying and recording, whether electronic or mechanical,
now known or hereinafter invented without permission in writing from the publisher.

www.JoAnnMDickinsonAuthor.com

ISBN: Hardcover 979-8-9885827-2-4
Paperback 979-8-9885827-3-1

The content of this work, including, but not limited to, the accuracy of events, people, and places
depicted; per mission to use previously published materials including; and any advice given or actions
advocated are solely the responsibility of the author, who assumes all liability for said work and
indemnifies the publisher against any claims stemming from publication of the work.

Two Sweet Peas Publishing

Amelia Ophelia
and Narwally
Protectors of the Sea

Written by JoAnn M. Dickinson
Illustrated by Kerrie Nichols

In the **sparkling** blue sea,
living happy and free,
was the friendliest narwhal —
content as can be.

And Narwally, that **whale**,
loved to swim every day
with his fellow cetaceans
who wanted to play.

Well, the order, cetaceans, has **porpoises**, too,
With the dolphins and narwhals, they're such a **fun crew!**
Because **narwhals** develop a tusk on their head,
they're called '**sea unicorns**,' which is truly well said!

NARWHAL

tail or flukes ⟶

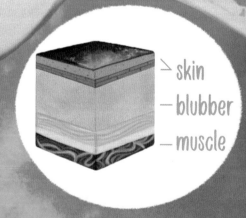

⟩ skin
— blubber
— muscle

The whole class typed as **mammals** are warm-blooded creatures—
like humans and monkeys and whales that it features.

Some scientists focus on mammals like whales.
While some others like studying mollusks like snails.

blowhole

spiral tusk

flippers

Yet, **Monodontidae** piques a strong interest, indeed.
It's a **family** that's called 'the white whales.' What a breed!

There are only two creatures in that group of whales:
The beluga and narwhals— with interesting tales!

Knowing this, young **Amelia** arrived at the shore.
She adored the deep sea and would love to **explore!**

Sea **biologist** training was one of her dreams,
and to study the **whales** was among her grand schemes.

When Narwally could spot her,
he **swam** to the beach.
She was hoping to learn,
and he wanted to **teach**.

There were still lots of narwhals
around on that day
And Amelia was hoping
to keep it that way.

So, **Narwally** would give her
a tour of the sea.
Many **porpoises**, dolphins,
and whales, she would see.

As Amelia was awed by
the **wonders** she'd seen,
with Narwally, her guide,
she'd **explore** the whole scene.

Her keen **interest** in dolphins
and whales grew and grew.

So, Narwally went out
and **recruited** a crew.

Then, Amelia was **learning** much more than before to **protect** all the oceans—preserving Earth's core.

Ocean Clean-up

Recycle

Fish Responsibly

Reduce pollution

Respect
Habitat

Soon, his excellent team met Amelia to share
what the sea creatures needed from all humans who care.

Narwally still **meets** with Amelia each day.
They **swim** and explore, they keep finding their way.

She doesn't yet know
all the **research** she'll do.
But her 'mentor,' **Narwally,**
will help her get through!

Fun Facts

Marine Mammals (Cetaceans)
- **Cetaceans** are marine mammals like whales, dolphins, and porpoises.
- They live in the water but are warm-blooded, like humans.
- There are about 90 different kinds of cetaceans.

Narwhals
- **Narwhals** are small whales with a long tusk, found in the Arctic.
- The tusk can be up to 10 feet long.
- They can live up to 50 years and often travel in groups.
- Narwhals are hunted by humans and other animals.

Porpoises
- **Porpoises** are small, dolphin-like creatures.
- They usually live for 8 to 10 years.
- They make noises called 'clicks' to talk and find things in the water.

Beluga Whales
- **Beluga Whales** are white and live in cold Arctic waters.
- They use sounds to talk and find things, using a special part of their head called a 'melon.'
- Belugas can live between 35 and 50 years.

Dolphins
- **Dolphins** are friendly and live in groups called schools.
- They make sounds to talk to each other.
- There are over 40 types of dolphins. The biggest one is the orca (killer whale).
- Orcas can live up to 90 years.

Types of Whales
- Some types of whales are humpback whales, blue whales, narwhals, orcas, beluga whales, and finback whales.
- The **North Pacific right whale** is very rare and one of the largest whale species.

Pronounciations

Monodontidae
mah-no-DON-tih-dye

Cetaceans
ce-ta-cean

Porpoises
por-poise

Mollusk
mol-lusk

JoAnn M. Dickinson is a multi-award-winning and best-selling author based in Southern California. Inspired by her grandchildren's love for nature and adventure, she began writing children's books in 2016. A few years later, JoAnn entered the world of self-publishing, releasing eight new titles, including the award-winning "Who's New at Lou's Zoo," was awarded Best Cover in 2022 and Book of the Year in 2023. Look for more new releases, including the upcoming "Amelia Ophelia Series." Discover delightful stories from JoAnn across her four series, all published by Two Sweet Peas Publishing.

Other books available:

Would you like to schedule an author visit?
Ask your teacher or librarian to email her:
JoAnn@JoAnnMDickinsonAuthor.com

Kerrie Nichols has been creating art since she could pick up a pencil. She continued to pursue her dream of illustrating and went to art school. From there she has taught art to kids in after-school programs, illustrated picture books, and taught elementary students for the last 12 years. Kerrie continues to use her colorful and whimsical illustrations and bring stories to life.

Made in the USA
Las Vegas, NV
18 October 2024

10059215R00021